MYSTERY AT POINT BEACH

Christmas Edition

~ Book 6 ~

Haunted Hemlock

Kate Jungwirth

Deborah Erdmann

Eternal Father, strong to save,

Whose arm does bind the restless wave,

Who bids the mighty ocean deep,

It's own appointed limits keep;

O hear us when we cry to Thee

For those in peril on the sea.

~

PROLOGUE

November 23rd, 1912

The ghostly tolling of a phantom bell sounded as the ship made her way along the dark waters of Lake Michigan near the shoreline of Two Rivers, Wisconsin.

Thousands of pine trees swayed on the deck as the ship rocked back and forth in the icy waves, creating the illusion of a floating forest.

The flag was flying at half-mast, nearly invisible in the thick fog that hovered overhead. Falling rain had turned into swirling vortexes of snow and ice in what would later be known as the "Greatest storm of the decade."

The ship had appeared out of nowhere and vanished just as quickly.

CHAPTER 1

I leaned sideways and breathed onto the icy truck window, which left a foggy patch on the glass. Not much different from the view of snow-covered trees going by in a blur as GB (my nickname for Grandpa Bob) sped down the winding road in his brand-new Ford F150.

Forest reached past me and drew a smiley face with its tongue sticking out in the steamed circle.

"Hey, what gives?"

"Sorry, Dominic. Just feeling a little stir crazy." He leaned back and yawned.

Sailor was curled up next to Forest, sound asleep; little snores escaping here and there.

It was a long ride, all the way from Chicago where Forest and Sailor live. While we were there, Windsong, their hippie grandma, packed up the rest of her belongings to bring to Green Bay where she had moved in with GB after their shotgun wedding last summer.

They had pooled together their retirement savings and were looking to buy a cottage near Manitowoc County, where they lined up a few open houses in the area; one of which was a small cabin next to Point Beach.

Personally, I was rooting for this cabin, since the other cabins they were considering were in Brussels and Algoma. I couldn't stomach vacationing some place with names like those.

Forest leaned forward and yelled, "Are we there yet?" interrupting GB and Windsong's jaunty rendition of "Jingle Bells" from the front seat.

Windsong looked back at us and smiled. "Almost there. Are you boys excited for your Christmas vacation at Point Beach?"

I nodded. "I'm excited that we don't have to rough it in the Nimrod." Nimrod is GB's vintage popup that we usually take camping. Fortunately, this time around Windsong talked him into staying at the original light keeper's dwelling next to the Rawley Point Lighthouse that was now used as a vacation rental. It was more romantic, she said. And being by the lake in the winter was a plus. She had GB wrapped around her pinky finger.

"Will the Buckleys already be there?" I asked.

"Sure hope so." GB looked at me through the rear-view mirror. "Bert has the keys."

Bert and Sadie Buckley were the annual camp hosts at Point Beach campground. As a gift for solving crimes at the park, they invited us to spend Christmas with them on the lake.

When we arrived at the office, I worried we'd be greeted by Ranger Rick, our nemesis at the campground, but it was closed for the holiday. *Sweet!* GB drove right on through to the lighthouse which was stationed near the beach.

"Are we there yet?" Sailor finally came to life, her nose pressing against the window.

"We're here, sweet pea." Windsong reached back, brushing the blonde bangs from Sailor's eyes.

A blast of cold air stung my face as I exited the truck.

"Brrr!" Windsong zipped up her fur-covered jacket and GB donned his wool watch cap.

Forest and I grabbed our duffle bags from the back of the truck while Sailor tugged at her magenta leopard-print suitcase from beneath the luggage pile.

The white lighthouse was majestic in stature. The light at the top of the steel tower began flashing as we went up the steps to the porch and made our way inside the three-story brick house.

"Helloooo!" Windsong's voice echoed through the corridor.

Sadie Buckley came to greet us, wiping her hands on her Rudolph the Reindeer apron. The aroma of peanut butter cookies followed her from the kitchen.

GB quizzically glanced around the room. "Where's Bert?"

Sadie pointed toward the lighthouse. "Oh, he's up in the tower, fiddling around. Some nonsense about getting ready to see the ghost ship from the old

Christmas tree shipwreck years ago." She shook her head. "You can ask him about that. I'm sure he'll have plenty to say."

As she gave us a tour of the inside and pointed upstairs to where the bedrooms were, a small white poodle scampered into the hall, letting out a few high-pitched yelps.

"Sprinkles, look who's here to visit!" Mrs. Buckley took the miniature poodle in her arms and rubbed noses with her. "I wub you, wub you, wub you!"

"Ugh, she's making me nauseous," Forest groaned.

"You can throw up later. For now, let's get unpacked so we can check out the place," I said. The three of us raced upstairs.

Sailor stopped on the second floor and entered the light green room with laced curtains. "I call dibs on this one!"

Forest and I went up one more level to the top of the tower. This room had a bunk bed and three windows that faced different directions, with a clear view of the lake, the woods, and the lighthouse. It would do nicely.

"Oh, no," I groaned as I looked in my duffle bag.

"What's up?" Forest climbed to the top bunk and rested back on his elbows.

"I forgot to pack underwear!"

"Don't sweat it, Dominic. Just follow the three-day rule."

"What's that?"

"Forward, backward, and inside out."

I threw a tennis shoe at his head and missed. "That's disgusting!"

By the time we had finished unpacking, I was ravenous. Forest and I ventured back to the ground floor. "What's to eat?" I said to no one in particular as I walked past the living room on my way to the kitchen.

GB looked up from behind the TV, where he was adjusting the antennae. "My stomach is rumbling. Can you hear it from there?"

"Oh, Bobby!" Windsong laughed. "How about a cheese pizza?"

I groaned. "Can we have meat, just this once?" Windsong's vegetarian diet was cramping my style.

"Guess what, wise guy?" She tousled my hair. "I brought a pepperoni one just for you."

"Now yer talkin'!" Forest walked into the room and dropped into a leather recliner next to the TV.

Windsong set down her knitting needles and headed for the kitchen. "Sailor," she yelled upstairs, "help me set the table!"

"Okay, Windsong!" Sailor called down.

By the time we had our fill of pizza and a vegetable salad that Sadie whipped up, the sun began setting, turning the sky above Lake Michigan into a kaleidoscope of reds and oranges.

"What say we have a fire by the lake?" Bert waited for a response to his bizarre idea.

GB shrugged. "I'm game. Who's on hot chocolate duty?"

So, there we sat, in the dark, in the freezing cold snow … like idiots.

It got quiet as we stared at the burning logs. I'm

sure we each had our own memories from the past few years camping here, but for me, my thoughts drifted off to the mysteries we had solved at Point Beach.

Windsong pulled a book from her satchel. "Kids, since we're staying in this historical lighthouse, I thought we should learn about its history."

She opened a book, titled, *Wisconsin's Haunted Lighthouses* and began reading.

Keeper Andrew J. Allen, who was in charge of the station from 1889 to 1895, wrote the district inspector in 1892 announcing that his assistant had quit. "Mr. John F. Craig quit today…on account of him and me could not get along…he would not obey my orders or take my advice." After settling at the station, Craig telegraphed for his "wife" in Kansas to join him. After she arrived, Keeper Allen noted, "Her mail came by the name of Carrie Spencer.

"Last evening," Keeper Allen continued, "they commenced to dance jigs which shook the plaster and when ordered to stop they said they would do just as they pleased, but I stopped them. This morning I asked

him to explain their conduct and character. He said he would quit, and I told him the quicker the better because I could not allow such doings. When he first came, he wanted to gamble with cards, but I would not have it done so long as I am Keeper."

"He sounds pretty strict," Sailor said.

"Does that remind you of someone we know?" Forest whispered.

I nodded. He was referring to Ranger Rick.

"Those were some real shenanigans; I tell you what." Bert gulped his hot chocolate a little too quickly, wincing in pain.

Windsong peered at us over the top of the book. "Now, don't be scared, but it says here that John Craig and Carrie Spencer haunt the lighthouse to this day. People reported hearing music and laughter in the middle of the night."

"Cool!" Forest said. "Another mystery for you to solve, Dominic." He patted me on the back, which made my cup of hot chocolate spill onto the ground. I crushed the empty cup with my boot.

"Interesting ..." Windsong turned the page. "It also says here there was a fire in 1962. The keeper's quarters were greatly damaged. One coastguardsman was severely burned, and three families were forced to evacuate. The 16-year-old son of one of the families was thought to have died in the fire. They never found his remains."

It got eerily quiet. As I stared at the frothy waves rolling onshore, my mind expanded, almost merging into the dark, cavernous sky that loomed overhead. I hadn't planned on encountering ghosts, but it sounded like the chances were good.

Sadie poked Bert. "Do you want to tell everyone the real reason we're holed up in the lighthouse in the dead of winter?"

Bert cleared his throat. "There was a shipwreck years ago, the Rouse Simmons, otherwise known as 'The Christmas Tree Ship.' It traveled back and forth from Chicago to Michigan every year, bringing ever-green trees from the north woods. They even called Captain Herman Schuenemann, 'Captain Santa.'"

He leaned forward in his seat, warming his hands over the fire. "In 1912 the ship disappeared in a storm, never to be seen again. That is, until local folks started claiming they saw visions of the ghost ship on Christmas Eve every year like clockwork."

Sadie shivered, pulling her wool scarf around her neck. "Do you see what I have to put up with?" She grimaced at Bert. "Old man and some foolish legend about phantom ships."

GB stood up. "Do you want to know what I think?"

"If we say yes, do you still have to tell us?" I asked.

"Very funny, Dominic." He folded up his chair. "I think it's time we hit the sack."

That night I had trouble sleeping—probably from the visions of sugar plums dancing in my head. Either that or the pizza. As I stared out the window at the full moon floating above the lake, I thought I heard music playing over the loud howling of the wind.

It sounded like a fiddle.

CHAPTER 2

Goosebumps rose on my skin. The strange sound I heard coming from down the hall reminded me of the story Windsong was reading about the past lighthouse keepers. Were John Craig and Carrie Spencer haunting the lighthouse? I imagined they played fiddles back in the day.

I grabbed my bathrobe from the hook next to the door and ventured into the hallway. The sound became louder as I approached Bert and Sadie's bedroom. I stood and listened by the door.

"Albert," Sadie groaned, "your alarm clock is going off. It's 4:00 am! Hit the snooze."

The bed squeaked. Sounded like Bert finally woke up. "The ship might be here!"

Not wanting to blow my cover, I hastily tip-toed back to my room.

I had finally fallen back into a restless sleep,

when I thought I heard fiddle music again. This time it was coming through the heat register from the basement, but I was too tired to investigate. After a few minutes it stopped, and I fell back asleep.

When the sun finally peeked through the light blue curtains, I sat up in bed and looked outside. The lake was a strange grey color, with icy edges forming at the shore.

Over a hearty breakfast of homemade granola and strawberries, we planned the day's activities.

Sailor slurped her last spoonful of cereal. "Hey, who was laughing last night?"

We all looked at each other.

"Maybe you were dreaming," Forest said.

"No, it woke me up." She glanced around the table. "I swear!"

"It's okay, honey. Sometimes things go bump in the night." Sadie reached for the coffee pot.

Bert started to say something, when Sadie threw him a warning look and quickly changed the subject.

"Say, kids. I thought it would be nice if you decorated the place. There's an artificial tree in the basement, and if you want to pick up some Christmas lights from the store, you could even decorate the tree out front." She winked at Windsong. "Wouldn't that put us in a festive mood?"

Perfect! That way we could buy red and green lights, and not the pink flamingo kind that Sadie decorates their campsite with every summer.

"That's a fine idea," Windsong agreed. "But first we do need to stop in at a cabin that's for sale just north of here. The owner is going to give us a tour."

"Is her name Audrey?" Sadie began gathering the empty plates. "We heard she hasn't been feeling well."

"Humpf. My wife just doesn't want to tell you why it's really for sale," Bert butted in. "Rumor is—that lady sees dead people."

Forest gave me the "look," but no one else seemed to take Bert seriously.

GB folded his newspaper. "Well, I don't see much else in the real estate section. So, I guess the haunted house is all we've got for today." He gulped down the remainder of his black coffee. "Let's hit the road."

It was a quick five-minute drive to the cabin. GB followed Highway O, slowing down when he spotted the "for sale" sign posted in front.

Tall, lanky hemlock trees lined both sides of the road. In the distance stood the rustic cabin, smoke curling from the chimney of the cedar roof. It was decked out for the holidays. Red and green lights hung from the entry way, with decorated planters on either side.

GB parked the truck as we stared at the property.

"Oh, Bobby, just look at this place—it's perfect!" Windsong's eyes lit up.

A middle-aged woman with brunette hair twisted up in a clip came out to greet us. "Well, hi there! I'm so glad you made it out in this weather." She drew her shawl around her shoulders. "You've come a long way."

GB reached her first. "Audrey, I presume?"

She nodded.

"I'm Bob Dorsey, and this is my wife, Windsong, and our grandkids, Dominic, Forest and Sailor."

We scrambled out of the truck.

"I can't wait to show you this place. It's been completely renovated—you're going to *love* it!" Her eyes sparkled.

Her enthusiasm rubbed off. Entering the cabin, it seemed that Windsong and GB liked what they saw. Everything was furnished with an artistic touch.

"I could move in right now. The scenery is magnificent." Windsong gazed through one of the oversized matching windows and pointed. "What's that in back of the cottage?"

"What? Do you see something?" Audrey nervously peered over her shoulder.

"It looks like a sunroom or a greenhouse?" Windsong clarified.

"Oh, yes." Audrey's voice relaxed. "That's where I keep my herb garden. I was just about to show you." She proudly waved her hand toward a door off the kitchen leading to a glass-enclosed room.

"Here's where I grow all the herbs that I use in my teas and other homemade recipes. It's one of my new hobbies." She shrewdly smiled, as though somehow this was her calling in life.

As she opened the service door, a wave of humidity poured out, mixed with an earthy, flowery scent. Dried lavender hung in bunches on the wall. Potting tables and shelves full of flower boxes and trays containing different varieties of strange, leafy plants lined the sides. I had no clue how anyone could distinguish one from the other.

"This is lovely, Audrey." Windsong slowly walked through the greenhouse, pausing to sniff each plant. "Though I don't consider myself an expert, I did learn about horticulture in my younger days, while living at a commune in California."

Yet another piece of the puzzle in the life of a gypsy.

Windsong stopped to study a plant in the corner. "What's this one with the green stem and purple-spotted bottom?"

Audrey approached the plant and stooped toward it, nearly pressing her nose to a cluster of tiny white flowers as she tried to breathe in the aroma.

"Why, this is Queen Anne's lace. It makes excellent jelly." She plucked a stalk from the pot. "I also have a lovely tea recipe. Would you care to sample it?" She held the herb toward Windsong, who took on an uneasy expression before backing away.

"I'm sorry, but are you sure this is Queen Anne's lace?" She nervously glanced at me and GB. "Because I have to say … this looks exactly like hemlock."

"Oh … so it is! My goodness. I did not plant that!" Audrey's eyes darted between GB and Windsong before resting on the plant. "I know the difference between Queen Anne's lace and hemlock!"

She studied the plant. "Strange. This pot is right where my Queen Anne's lace was sitting."

Just a hunch, but if she was drinking tea from this plant, that would explain why she was seeing dead people.

Suddenly, she jumped as though she saw a ghost. Wiping sweat from her brow, she nervously glanced at us. "Did you see that?" she whispered, pointing to a shadow in the corner.

We turned our heads in the direction she pointed to. A white Persian cat with hypnotic blue eyes leaped out from behind a flowerpot.

"Socrates!" she yelled at the cat. "Bad boy!"

The cat meowed and scampered behind a row of bagged potting soil.

"Audrey, this cabin is perfect!" Windsong said. "It's right in the woods, and close to Point Beach, our favorite stomping ground." She winked at us.

Audrey blushed. "I was hoping you'd like it. I had a feeling this would be a good fit for you."

GB rubbed his chin. "May I ask why you're selling?"

"It's a long story," she began. "My grandfather built this cabin after he and my grandmother married. They raised their two sons here. After they passed on, the cabin was left to me. Grandfather knew it would be in good hands." She lifted her chin. "I'm an aspiring artist. The natural setting sparks my creativity."

Windsong patted her on the back. "I'm sure your

grandfather would be very proud of you."

"Yes, I'm sure he would approve." She brushed away a lock of dark brown hair that escaped her updo. "I've studied the work of the local artist Two Rivers native, Lester Bentley, for some time now. He's a distant relative, in fact. I've been toying with the idea of following in his footsteps and attending the Art Institute of Chicago — Bentley's Alma Mater."

Windsong put a hand over her heart. "I grew up in Chicago. I have admired Bentley's artwork for many years."

Audrey's face flushed. "We're kindred spirits, my dear." She patted Windsong's shoulder. "So, anyway, I feel if I don't get there soon, I'll go out of my mind."

Too late for that.

"But where are my manners. Let me show you the rest of the place."

We followed her into the living room. The modern design was simplistic yet high-class. I approved of Audrey's taste. The elevated ceilings sloped down toward large, framed windows with white spacious walls featuring framed pieces of art.

"Don't you love the wood-burning fireplace?" She pointed out the copper edging, but my attention shifted to a painting hung above the mantle.

It was of a middle-aged man with deep auburn hair and a curled mustache. The piercing black eyes seemed to be following me. Eerie as all get-out. Not to mention the elegant, engraved ceramic urn that sat next to it.

Audrey followed my gaze.

"I should explain ..." she looked at the floor and continued, her voice strained. "My uncle Vincent died in a terrible accident five years ago. I was the last living relative, so it fell to me to preserve his honor."

Windsong covered her mouth with her hand. "I'm so sorry, Audrey."

"Thank you. But at least his final resting place is the cabin that he grew up in. And there's a memorial stone at the small cemetery down the road. I plan on visiting later today, before we get the 6" of snow that's predicted for tonight."

As we headed out, a pickup truck pulled into the driveway. A gaunt, white-haired man wearing overalls stepped out of the truck and yanked a beat-up toolbox from the back seat. He slammed the door and turned, looking startled to see us.

Audrey approached him. "Good morning, Hank."

He looked at her like she had two heads, muttering something unintelligible before heading into the cabin.

"I call him 'cantankerous Hank.' Good help is hard to find nowadays, so I had to resort to hiring the lighthouse groundskeeper." She must've noticed the concern on GB and Windsong's faces. "Now don't you worry yourselves. He's just rewiring a few lights in the basement. Other than that, the cabin is in excellent condition."

She walked us out. "In case you want to come back for another look, I keep a spare key here." She pulled up a fake rock from under a front window.

"Thank you, Audrey! We'd better get going. We need to run to Two Rivers to buy Christmas lights and ornaments and pick up some underwear for Dominic."

Ugh … she just had to go there.

Audrey nodded. "While you're at it, might I suggest stopping by Schroeder's Department Store? They keep a display of my paintings." She lowered her voice. "A few of them were stolen, but my good friend Julia is keeping a careful watch on what's left. With the robberies and a few ghost sightings being investigated besides, it's most untimely for the holidays."

Were the ghosts of Christmas past paying a visit? I shivered at the thought.

CHAPTER 3

As we drove away from the cabin, Forest, Sailor and I huddled together in the back seat, waiting for the heater to kick in. GB reached for the radio dial and tuned in to a local station.

"So, let me get this straight. Not only do you have proof that aliens from outer space exist, but you also have evidence of ghost encounters?" A man with a deep, baritone voice questioned.

"That's correct. Ghosts, aliens — they're all interconnected. It seems Wisconsin is a hot spot for paranormal activity."

This voice sounded oddly familiar.

"Turn it up, GB — I want to hear this!"

GB cranked it up as the interviewer continued.

"Well, that's all the time we have for this unusual segment of 'Be My Guest,' on WOMT. Once again, we would like to thank Quinn, the founder of SCI-FI-WI, for

joining us today. Be sure to follow his YouTube documen-tary as he investigates Two Rivers' ghost sightings in the upcoming episode."

"Hey, no problem, dude. Like I said, if there's a ghost in this town, I'll find it."

"Good luck with that … but in any case, we'd love to have you back on the show."

"It would be my pleasure. Live long and prosper. Nanu, Nanu."

I could hardly contain myself. "Hey, guys, did you hear that? It's Quinn. He's back in Two Rivers!"

"Yeah, we heard." Forest looked up from his phone. "The website says he's going to be shooting a video at Schroeder's Department Store in about an hour. Perfect timing. Can we go? Please?"

"Is that the odd fella with all the radar antennas sticking out of his van?" GB asked.

"Oh, yeah, now I remember," Windsong recalled. "He was camping at Point Beach the year when the Buckleys insisted the park was being invaded by aliens. That was a blast!"

"♪ If there's something strange … in your neighborhood … who you gonna call? ♪" Sailor sang.

"Ghostbusters!" Forest high-fived her.

I was thrilled by the chance to meet up with Quinn again, but it was the thought of seeing a ghost that really raised my spirits.

By the time we picked up a few sets of tree lights, Christmas ornaments and Fruit of the Loom, the sun had begun to set.

GB parked outside the Schroeder's building.

Around the corner, I spotted the green under-glow of Quinn's van coming down the road. The streetlights reflected the scanner antennas as they swayed back and forth, with a mobile satellite dish rotating in circles against the darkened sky.

Quinn spotted us as he got out. "Hey, kids! What are you doing here?" He nodded at GB and Windsong as he pulled up his fur-lined camouflage hood.

Sailor ran up to him. "We need to get rid of a ghost that's hanging around this cabin near Point Beach." She threw a few karate chops at an invisible opponent.

Quinn shook his head in amusement. "You really are a weird little bird."

"We know there's usually a logical explanation," I interrupted, "but after hearing your radio interview, we felt an investigation was in order to make sure these sightings are legit."

"Yeah, could we tag along to see what we might be dealing with in case Two Rivers really is haunted?" Forest asked.

"Sounds like this will be right up your alley. I already picked up a strong disturbance on my radar." Quinn opened the sliding door on the side of the van, revealing a row of monitors.

"Besides, I could use a new wingman," Quinn said, reminding me that we had sent his crony associate to jail the last time we met when we thought Point

Beach was being overrun by illusionary aliens.

Quinn handed me his video camera, then reached for what looked like a small yellow and black radar gun which he called an "EMF meter," and a black backpack.

We followed Quinn into the building. Ghost or no ghost, some electric heat would hit the spot right about now. The aroma of roasting coffee beans greeted us at the door.

"We're going to stop at the Red Bank for a hot drink and read the paper while we wait." GB grabbed Windsong's hand as they headed toward the small coffee shop in the front of the store.

Just as well. GB doesn't believe in ghosts.

Quinn approached a middle-aged man, nicely dressed in a checkered wool vest over a button-down shirt who stood behind the counter.

"Hello, Sir. I'm here to investigate ghost sightings. Could I talk to Mr. Schroeder?"

He raised an eyebrow. "I'm sorry, but he's passed on."

Quinn scratched his head. "In that case, can I talk to Mrs. Schroeder?"

"I'm afraid she has passed on, too." He eyed our group suspiciously from behind a stack of shoe boxes.

Forest stepped up to the man and raised his hands. "Is there anyone we can talk to who's not dead?"

Just then, a woman dressed in jeans and a turtleneck sweater approached us. She had black-rimmed cat eyeglasses which made her look more like a librarian than a clerk.

"Well, hello!" She beamed at the sight of us. "I'm Julia. You must be the ghostbusters. It's a good thing you're here. The more ghost sightings we get, the fewer customers."

The shoe salesman nodded in agreement. "Hi, I'm Glen." His eyes widened behind wire glasses. "I can tell you all about the ghost I saw a few years ago."

"You're up, Dominic." Quinn turned on the video camera and hit "RECORD" as I stayed focused on Glen through the viewfinder.

"I'll never forget the day Mr. Schroeder died." The man stared intently into the camera. "I vividly remember going upstairs to take a few shoe boxes out of storage, when I noticed a bright glow. That's when I saw his ghost eating a tuna fish sandwich."

A ghost that eats tuna? Sounded fishy to me.

"Ah, yes … tuna was his favorite." Julia rolled her eyes. "Thank you, Glen."

"Interesting." Quinn adjusted the backpack straps on his shoulder. "I'll add that to my research. Now, if it's okay with you, my crew and I would like to take a look around."

Just then, Glen's cell phone rang. He slipped the phone out of his pocket, glanced back at us and headed down the hallway, lowering his voice to a whisper as he spoke to the caller.

"Well, gang, perhaps we should we start in the basement." Julia directed us down the staircase into a miniature version of Toyland.

Nothing strange appeared among the rows of games and toys in this part of the store, but as soon as she opened a heavy metal door leading to the rest of the basement, the atmosphere suddenly shifted. The dingy walls, stale smell, and lack of proper lighting made our surroundings rather creepy.

Quinn kept an eye on the EMF reader as we covered the entire floor. "So far, there hasn't been any fluctuation of electromagnetic energy. Maybe we'll have better luck where Glen saw Mr. Schroeder's ghost. Can you take us there next?" he asked Julia.

"As you wish." She led us to the elevator on the far end of the building. The door slid open revealing an old steel box that looked like a coffin. As Julia hit the button for the second floor, it turned fluorescent green, casting an eerie glow throughout the confined space.

The elevator jolted as it slowly made its way up. At the top, we stepped into a large room full of empty clothes racks, reams of paper, boxes, and packaging material.

"This is the spot. The ghost was sitting right over there." Julia pointed to a plaid upholstered armchair. "Have a look around. I need to head back down to start closing up for the night," she said as she returned to the elevator.

The door closed behind her and the vibration of the steel cables extending down the elevator shaft made the overhead lights flicker and the floor shake.

Sailor took a step backward, bumping into what at first glance looked like a faceless person. She placed a hand over her heart, taking a deep breath. "Oh — thank goodness it's only a mannequin!"

"Yeah, but in the dark, it looks like a ghost," I said.

The collection of white, doll-like statues that lined the wall behind us freaked me out, but I didn't let on. I kept focused on Quinn.

"I'm not getting much of anything over here." He passed the EMF reader over the chair a few times. "But keep recording, Dominic. The ghost of Mr. Schroeder is going to need to rest sooner or later."

I nodded and zoomed in the lens on the chair, noticing something white stuck between the cushions. I reached down to grab what seemed to be a folded-up piece of paper and quickly shoved it in my pocket before realizing that everyone had left the room.

I caught up to Quinn who was already halfway down a long corridor with Forest and Sailor. At the other end, we entered a room with mosaic tiled flooring, vibrant wallpaper, and crafted woodwork. Old books sat on a crowded shelf next to an examination table.

"Pay attention, space cadets." Quinn began to scan the room. "Here's where Dr. Zlatnik's office used to be. Eyewitnesses swear they saw his ghost through the window, rummaging around in here at night."

Out of the corner of my eye, I caught sight of a pale hand reaching over my shoulder and instantly froze.

"Ahh, look behind you!" Sailor shrieked, backing up into the corner. "It's a ghost!"

I brushed the stiff white hand away and spun around to find Forest with a smirk on his face, holding up a fake arm from one of the mannequins.

I was ready to clobber him with it, when suddenly there was a crackling sound. The lights dimmed a few times, then went out. The room became pitch black and deathly quiet—except for Sailor's whimpering.

"Nice job, Forest—you woke up the ghost of Dr. Zlatnik!" she sobbed.

"Are you kidding me?" I tried to keep the video camera steady while shaking uncontrollably.

"Guess we lost power." Quinn handed Forest a flashlight. "On the upside, I just took a thermal reading and there's a cold draft circulating. This could be it!"

Sailor grabbed Forest's arm, squeezing tightly.

I have to admit, I wasn't a fan of the dark, either. Especially when I didn't know my way around.

"Don't worry, we only have a little more ground to cover. Dominic, let me know if you see anything." Quinn switched the camera to night vision.

Nothing out of the ordinary showed up, but all the while, I had a feeling that someone was watching us.

As the group ventured back out into the hall, I stopped at one of the double-paned windows and lifted the roller shade. Light snow softly fell amid the streetlights and the cars lining the parking spaces were sparse as the town prepared to shut down for the night.

I suddenly felt a brush of cold air on the back of my neck. Out of nowhere, a luminous image formed on the other side of the glass. *What in the world was that?*

CHAPTER 4

Looking through the camera's viewfinder, I was startled by the strange glowing orb that unexplainably manifested outside the window. It hovered only a few yards away by what appeared to be a pair of wings.

The translucent figure held me in a trance before taking flight.

"Guys!" I took a few steps back from the windowsill. "I think I just saw a ghost!"

Forest and Sailor ran through the doorway and stopped dead in their tracks. A shriek erupted from the radiator, like steam escaping from a kettle.

As it quieted, I uncovered my ears and heard a chilling voice repeat, *"Leave me alone ..."*

No one dared to make a sound. Forest pointed his flashlight toward a vent that ran along the floor's baseboards where the wispy voice had emerged.

The overhead lights crackled as they powered

back on. We found ourselves alone in the room, but the experience left us terrified.

"There you are." Quinn stepped in front of the doorway. "I don't mean to rush anyone, but the weather is worsening." He glanced out the window, the same one the ghost disappeared from.

"Get me outta here!" Sailor blubbered. "The ghost is after us."

"What ghost?" Quinn asked.

"It was here a minute ago," I stammered. "There was a strange glowing orb outside the window and then a voice came from out of nowhere telling us to leave. Forest and Sailor heard it too."

"Whoa!" Quinn's eyes widened. He held out a special tool that looked like a revolving metal ice cream scooper. "Nothing's here now, but tomorrow I'll take a look at the video footage and see what shows up."

As he escorted us toward a wide staircase, I grabbed hold of the railing leading back down to a loft overlooking the main floor. We found Julia behind a cluttered desk and a row of filing cabinets, in the process of placing something heavy into a black, full-sized metal vault that was built into the wall.

"Well … did you find our ghost?" She shut the door and reset the combination lock with a spin of the numbered dial after she saw us coming.

"We found something, alright," Quinn said, "but whether or not it's an actual ghost remains to be seen."

"Super! Let me know if you need anything else for the documentary." Julia stepped away from the vault. "Just securing a few valuable paintings by a local artist, Audrey Hart. Do you know her? She owns a cabin near Point Beach."

"As a matter of fact, we do. Our grandparents are considering buying that cabin," I replied.

Julia nervously bit her lip. "I should probably warn you. Audrey is not in her right mind. I would tread carefully."

And with that, we made our way out.

"Small world!" Quinn said, as he pulled up his hood and headed toward his van. "What are the chances you both know the same lady?"

"This is Two Rivers, not Chicago." Forest shook his head.

"I'll be in touch." Quinn saluted.

The lighthouse was dark as we pulled into the driveway. The Buckleys must've turned in for the night. We quietly made our way to our sleeping quarters. Forest grabbed his phone and settled into his bunk.

Good idea. I reached into my backpack for my phone to check my messages, when my hand brushed against the paper I had found at Schroeder's. I shined my cellphone light on it and saw a hand-written list:

Schroeder's

Library

Hemlock Lane

Rawley Point

Hmm. A list of local establishments, and if I remembered right, Audrey's cabin was on Hemlock Lane.

I was just dozing off when a shadow cast in front of the window shook me to the core.

It was Forest.

"Dominic!" He ran to the window and motioned for me to take a look.

I joined him at the window. "Just what exactly are we looking for in the middle of the night?"

"I woke up to the sound of the floorboards creaking on the stairs. I froze at first, but when no one came in, I couldn't fall back asleep, so I got up and stretched." He pointed to the tower. "I saw a man dressed in black. He was carrying a big box. I think he was trying to get into the tower building."

"Just to confirm. You saw a man … in the dark … dressed in black. Are you sure you weren't dreaming?" I rubbed my eyes.

"Did I mention … he had a hat with a flashlight attached?" Forest crossed his arms.

"Okay. Okay. Should we go outside and check it

out? If it turns out to be a ghost, we'll score big with Quinn."

"Not tonight." Forest closed the curtain and yawned. "I'm exhausted. First thing in the morning."

"Um, okay. Thanks for the wake-up call."

The next morning the aroma of cinnamon French toast wafted up the stairs. I had planned on sleeping in, but my appetite calls the shots. By time I got dressed and combed my hair, Forest had rolled out of bed and joined me.

Sadie was up bright and early, shuffling around the kitchen in her pointed-toe elf slippers, her blue hair wrapped in rollers. If that wasn't enough to make sure we were fully awake, I don't know what was.

"Well, howdy doody, boys! You're up bright and early." She beamed at us as she placed a bottle of maple syrup on the table. The aroma must have woken everyone up. GB, Windsong and Sailor came drifting in. Only one person was missing.

"Where's Bert?" I asked, as I settled into a chair at the end of the table.

Sadie frowned. "That old fart. Stayed up half the night looking for the ghost ship. Now he's out like a light. It's two days until Christmas. The rumor is the ship comes on Christmas and not before. But that's Bert."

GB reached for a mug of coffee. "You know what they say, he who waits for Santa never sees him."

"Lands, yes. Well, let's eat!" Sadie unfolded a napkin over her lap.

After breakfast, the plan was for Forest and me to look for footprints in the snow. So, when Windsong handed us the box of Christmas lights to decorate the big pine tree out front, it was the perfect opportunity.

"I get to put the star on top!" Sailor yelled as we headed out.

That was fine by me. Let her decorate the tree while Forest and I survey the scene.

I pulled the strings of my hoodie tight and braced myself. Wisconsin winters are nothing to mess around with. This isn't called the "frozen tundra" for nothing. We started walking in the diamond-crusted snow.

"Hey, Forest." I pulled him aside, "Do you think Bert might've seen the man in black? He was up in the middle of the night looking for a ghost ship."

"Maybe. We can ask him if he ever wakes up."

Sailor raced to the tree with the box of lights clutched under her arm. "Come on, guys! Aren't you going to help me?"

"Um. Yeah. But first … we have to look at these footprints. Maybe Santa came early."

"Ooh, let me help!" She dropped the box and began helping us look.

"Try over there." I misdirected her while Forest and I went off on our own.

"Bingo!" Forest pointed to a set of large snow-shoe prints.

It looked like they came from the woods and

went right to the lighthouse tower. The prints stopped at the tower and disappeared. Was someone still inside? We tried the door, but it was locked.

"Guess we met a dead end." I sighed.

After 10 minutes of walking around aimlessly, Sailor shouted, "Look at these prints! Someone's boots left behind a star shape in the snow. It had to be Santa!"

Intrigued, Forest and I started following the star prints.

"Ughh, you idiot!"

I turned to Forest to see what the problem was.

"Sailor, look at the bottom of your boots."

She tipped up a boot and we studied it.

"Your boots have stars on the bottom!" Forest shoved her into a snowbank.

I reached out a hand to help her up.

"Well, that was a big waste of time. Let's put the lights on the tree before our fingers get frostbite."

We had nearly finished, when a flinty, high-pitched voice interrupted.

"Hold it right there!" It was Ranger Rick. He was dressed in a snowsuit with a fur-lined hood and snow-shoes on his feet. "Just what do you think you're do-ing?"

Forest dropped the string of lights.

"This is government property, Illi-noyance. Santy Claus doesn't make the rounds at state parks." His steamed breath made a cloud in the cold air.

Kwitch … "Honey bear, what's your 20? Got a cup of joe with your name on it," crooned a female voice over the ranger's walkie-talkie.

Ranger Rick's face turned bright red. Could've been frost bite, but I doubt it. Everyone knew he was sweet on Ranger Sally.

"What are you kids doing here this time of year?"

"We're here with the Buckleys, hoping to see the ghost of the Christmas Tree ship!" Sailor blurted out.

Forest and I glared at her, but it was no use.

"That old ghost ship? No such thing as ghosts … and no Santa either!" He shook his finger at us. "Stay inside, if you know what's good for you." And with that he marched off, stumbling over his snowshoes.

Could he be the man we saw last night?

We finished decorating the tree, not heeding the ranger's warning. It was Sadie Buckley's idea in the first place. Let her deal with the ranger.

We entered the house through the back door, leaving our boots and coats in the entryway.

Sadie was sitting at the kitchen table, sprinkling colored sugar on a pile of frosted Christmas cookies. I liked her blue nail polish. It matched the veins in her hands.

"Hey, kids! How does the tree look?"

"Ranger Rick yelled at us. He said there's no such thing as Santa Claus or a ghost ship." Sailor crossed her arms.

Sadie made a clucking sound. "Never you mind that old Grinch. He'll come around."

"Where's Bert?" I asked.

"He's up in the tower. Why don't you take a snack up to him?" She arranged a tray with cookies, a full cup of coffee, and creamer.

Forest and I carried the treats out to the tower while Sailor helped Sadie decorate the rest of the cookies. We walked beneath the web of metal supports toward the door that led inside.

"Is Mrs. Buckley nuts?" I took one look upward at the narrow spiral staircase and another at the tray of cookies and coffee that I was supposed to get to the top.

By the time we reached the main gallery deck, half of the coffee had spilt making the cookies a bit soggy. There stood Bert, his eyes glued to Lake Michigan.

"Hi, boys. Come join me. There's a storm brewing over the lake."

I set down the coffee and cookies and observed the darkening clouds churn above the water. The beacon of light from the lantern in the watch room reflected its turbulence with every rotation.

"The *Farmer's Almanac* is predicting strange weather patterns," Bert warned. "It's a resurgence of the 'Lake Michigan Triangle,' I tell you what. Ever hear about the Northwest Orient Airlines Flight 2501?"

"No, never." I shook my head.

"It flew into an electrical cloud and vanished—swept clean off the radar. Before long, the coast guard started to see ships disappear without a trace." Bert pursed his lips. "Just like Captain Santa trying to bring holiday cheer with his Christmas Tree Ship. Mark my words—it will happen again."

He helped himself to a cookie. "I know the Christmas Tree Ship sighting is still a few days away, but you have to be vigilant. You have to." As he bit into his cookie, a few crumbs landed in his lap.

Forest took over with the next question. "Did you happen to see any … um, activity on the property from your birds-eye view?"

"Such as?" Bert stirred creamer into his coffee.

"Like, did you see anyone walking around here in the middle of the night?"

Bert paused. "Well, now. I can't say that I did. But truth be told," he yawned, not bothering to cover his mouth, "truth be told, I did doze off, and so on and so forth and what have you, so it's possible I napped part of the night."

For an old geezer trying to cash in on a Christmas miracle, I'd have to say his ship wasn't coming in anytime soon.

CHAPTER 5

"Kids! There you are." GB and Windsong walked into the room. "We have an early Christmas present for you."

Windsong pulled out three identical green foil-wrapped packages from behind the couch and lined them up on the floor. "We know it's not Christmas yet, but why don't you go ahead and open these." She stood back, rubbing her hands together in anticipation.

I bent down to grab one of the gifts. By the looks of them, this was going to be something big!

Peeling back the paper held by tape, we each uncovered our very own set of cross-country skis with poles. Pink for Sailor, green for Forest, and blue for me — my favorite color.

"We thought these skis would be great for the trails." GB revealed three additional wrapped boxes which I assumed were boots.

"Gosh, thanks!" I gave each of them a hug.

"Hey, I have an idea," Windsong said. "Your grandpa and I are going over to the cabin soon. Why don't you use the skis and meet us there? You can take the nature trail all the way to the property line."

"Is it okay if I stay here?" Sailor asked. "Mrs. Buckley's going to teach me how to make snowflake ornaments for the tree."

"Sure, honey. I think it's a good idea to keep those old Christmas traditions." Windsong kissed Sailor on the top of her head.

Forest and I suited up and were out the door. I was relieved that Sailor decided to stay at the lighthouse. With her out of our hair, we could get things done.

The air felt crisp upon my cheeks, with only a hint of sunlight escaping through thick, grey clouds.

Thankfully, the wind was at bay which would've made any type of activity more exhausting.

I reached down to clip my boots into the bindings of my brand-new skis; rhythmically using the poles in time with my legs to glide along the freshly fallen powder that covered the trail.

Forest came up alongside me as we purposely lured each other on and off the trail onto some of the rougher terrain where the ridges and dunes were buried beneath the snow. Sometimes, if we hit it just right, our skis would pick up speed creating a few small jumps to go over.

Although I caught a lot of air, when I landed, one of my skis crossed the other and tripped me up. I face-planted right into the bank.

"Nice one, Dominic!" Forest teased.

Brushing off the snow, I stood back up a few feet from the road that bordered the property.

"Wow, I never realized how close the cottage is to the park." Through the trees, I could see the cabin; the smoke curling up out of the chimney. GB's truck was parked outside along with Audrey's SUV and Hank's work vehicle.

"Looks like company." Forest read my mind.

We removed our skis and propped them up against the side of the cottage along with our poles.

"Hi kids! Come on in. Audrey was kind enough to make us lunch." Windsong ushered us to the table.

Two teacups next to the plates contained colored liquids which looked intriguing. "What are those blue and purple drinks?" I leaned forward to take a whiff of the blue one. It smelled like wood.

Audrey took a seat. "It's butterfly pea flower tea. The tea is blue, but if you add a lemon wedge it turns violet. And if you add tonic water, it turns bright pink. Fabulous, isn't it?"

"Cool!" Forest leaned over one of the cups to get a closer look. "It's like a mood ring cocktail!"

Windsong smiled and sipped her tea. "So, tell me, how was the ski trail?"

"It was okay," I said. "Nothing out of the ordinary happened."

"Except for when Dominic decided to stop off and take a bath in the snow!" Forest jabbed me in the arm.

"Can I get you some cucumber sandwiches?" Audrey stood to her feet.

Cucumber? Forest mouthed the word to me.

"Ah, no thanks. We just had some … ah, pizza rolls."

"Pizza rolls! Where on earth did you get that?" Windsong raised an eyebrow.

"Um. Bert had some in his … lunch box."

Dang. I better leave the lying to Forest. He's much better at it.

Audrey shook her head in exasperation. "Sit down, you two." She began rummaging through the fridge before settling on an assortment of cheese and fruits which she set on the table.

When I sat down, Socrates came wandering into the kitchen and curled up at my feet. His warm fur helped to thaw the frost from under my socks.

As we ate our lunch, Audrey continued the conversation with Windsong that she was involved with before we arrived.

"So, like I was saying," she whispered loudly to Windsong, "the book came flying off the shelf, and landed on the floor right at my feet!" She held her hand over her mouth—her face turning an ashen white.

Windsong went to Audrey's side and rubbed her shoulder. "Honey, are you sure that really happened?"

"Yes! Yes, I'm sure. And don't blame the hemlock. I definitely did not put that dreadful stuff in my tea. But you won't believe what happened next—I saw Uncle Vincent!" Her eyes grew big as saucers. "I saw him, I tell you, right out that window." She pointed out the kitchen window that faced the woods.

"Queen Anne's lace aside, are you using any fresh herbs from your greenhouse in your tea? There are plenty of herbs that can cause hallucinations, such as the salvia plant family."

"Now, Windsong," Audrey's lip trembled, "I know you don't believe me, but I do know my plants. I go strictly by the book." She pointed to a row of individually labeled canisters on the counter.

"You can look for yourself. I dry each plant, and then grind them and store them in canisters, attaching a label with the date on it. All perfectly safe, I assure you."

I pulled Forest into the living room.

"What now?" he whispered.

"Just a hunch." I ran my hand along the edges of each of the six shelves of the bookcase. I didn't notice anything out of place.

"What, you believe that fruit cake?" Forest wrinkled his nose. "Don't tell me you're drinking the tea, too?"

"Not a fan." I lowered my voice. "To be honest, I believe her. She recognized the hemlock and swore she didn't plant it."

I walked over to the portrait of creepy Vinny that hung over the fireplace.

"I could've sworn those eyes followed me last time we were here." I ran my hand through my hair. "Listen, I know it seems over the top, but I have a feeling we were followed here. Not only that, with the artwork gone missing at Schroeder's, and since some of it is actually this lady's … well, something just seems … off."

I cut the conversation after being interrupted by the sound of boots stomping up the nearby steps.

"Well, you know, this old cabin looks great on the outside, but is it up to code on the inside?"

I recognized GB's voice.

"I'm well familiar with building codes," another voice said with a laugh.

That voice I didn't recognize. It must be Hank. The two men came up from the basement, GB with a tape measure and stud-finder in his hand.

"I didn't find any mold, but there seems to be a structural flaw in the crawl space," GB said.

"Sounds like the two of you are working up a thirst!" Audrey cheerfully greeted them. "Care to try an exotic butterfly tea?" She pointed to a glass pitcher on the counter, the blue and violet colors swirling.

"Is this tea made with plants from your garden?"

Hank carefully eyed the pitcher.

"Why, yes. Yes, it is. All my teas are home-grown," Audrey said.

Hank slowly backed away. "I have to be heading out. I finished the basement project. I noticed there's a few loose bricks around your foundation. We can talk about that later." He grabbed his jacket from the coat hook and quickly hurried out the front door.

"Hmpf." GB eyeballed Hank as he walked away. "I'm the one who noticed it while inspecting the basement."

"Well, he seems pleasant enough." Windsong pulled out a chair for GB. "What on earth were the two of you doing down there?"

"Just making sure the cabin is sturdy." GB leaned in for a closer look into the pitcher of tea. "There isn't anything in here I should worry about, is there?" he asked Audrey.

Luckily, she didn't seem to hear him.

"Bobby!" Windsong chuckled and playfully swatted at him with her napkin.

"To be honest," GB said, "Hank is very knowledgeable. We discussed the private land around here, and the history of how the area became established."

While everyone enjoyed tea and dessert, Forest and I excused ourselves. I said we were heading back to the lighthouse to help decorate the tree … *NOT!*

As we circled to the back of the house, Forest nearly tripped over a loose brick that stuck out from the foundation. He pushed the brick with his ski pole which caused another brick to come loose. That must be the area Hank was going to work on.

"Take it easy, Forest. Let's not wreck the place and ruin our chances to spend our summers here."

I put the bricks back as best as I could and noticed a boarded-up window behind them. Weird.

"So, what are we looking for?" Forest asked as we clumsily circled the cabin on our skis.

"Let's play devil's advocate." I leaned against a tree behind the house. "We had a few inches of snow last night, so if someone in fact was seen outside of the window, then there should be footprints."

My theory proved to be true. A set of large boot prints led from the kitchen window into the woods. I motioned for Forest to follow me.

As we tracked the footprints, my mind was busy focusing on clues. Audrey is an artist. Her pictures are stolen. She sees dead people. Meh. That went nowhere. The prints, on the other hand, led to something more.

"Snowmobile tracks!" I examined the caterpillar tread with two skis in front headed in the direction of Point Beach. "Let's see where they lead."

Gliding over the packed snow was easy, and just as I suspected, the trail went all the way to the light-house. This was strange. Why would someone spy on Audrey and then come here?

After removing our skis, we stepped up to the solid metal door that led into the tower, but it was locked.

"What now?" Forest hugged himself, trying to keep warm.

"Hey! Get away from there, you nosy kids!"

It was Hank. He planted his shovel into a

snowbank and grabbed us by our hoods.

"But we're guests here." I tried to reason with him.

Hank dropped back a few feet. "Guests or not, you should know it's not safe. Stay inside where you belong." He grabbed his shovel and disappeared around the building, leaving huge boot prints behind him.

"Wow, he was about to eat our lunch and pop the bag." Forest shook his head.

We moved our skis outside the porch door and headed in, where another unpleasant surprise awaited us. Make that two.

CHAPTER 6

Rangers Sally and Rick sat glumly on the couch, a pile of tangled lights at their feet. The same ones we had strung on the pine tree outside, I could only assume.

Bert and Sadie Buckley sat on the other side of the room; heads drooped.

"Oh, the tangled web we weave when first we practice to deceive." Ranger Rick's glare was piercing. "Just what did I tell you kids about those lights!"

"Now, Ricky," Sally patted his arm. "It's Christmas!"

"Bah humbug!" The ranger stood to his feet. "It's bad enough you're catting around here all summer long, but this is supposed to be my quiet time of the year." He stomped his foot for added effect. "Those lights are a fire hazard. You don't want to burn down the place, do you?"

"Oh, we understand, Officer Rick." Sadie said.

Forest looked at his feet. "Um, sure."

Sadie turned to the rangers, smiling brightly as she tousled the fuzzy ball on her Santa hat. "Could I interest you in a cup of hot cocoa?"

"No, Ma'am. We have to be heading out." Sally's smile made the wrinkles in the corners of her eyes deepen. "We surely do appreciate it, though!"

After the rangers got up to leave, Sadie turned to us. "Now, don't let the ranger's comments dampen your mood. I know just the thing to put you back in the Christmas spirit!"

She pointed to a plastic Charlie Brown Christmas tree in the corner. It was full of cobwebs and stunk like mildew.

"Windsong bought lights and ornaments for it. I'll put on some Bing Crosby Christmas tunes, and we'll have a merry old time decking the halls of this historic building!"

"Whoo! That sounds like fun, Mrs. B!" Sailor played right into her hands. She oohed and aahed over the shiny tinsel and trinkets.

Bert lit up his pipe and sat back to watch the decorating of the tree like it was a lavish theatrical production. After a while he got bored and reached for a newspaper, while Forest and I grabbed some snacks and settled in front of the TV to watch *How the Grinch Stole Christmas.*

That's one mystery we already solved.

GB and Windsong got back just in time for dinner. Sadie's roast chicken and mashed potatoes actually looked edible. We gathered hands to pray before digging in. Windsong filled up on a vegetable dish that she had microwaved, while Forest and I fought over a drumstick.

"Say, kids. How was your afternoon?" GB asked as he poured himself a glass of milk. "I see you found the Christmas tree." He winked at Sailor. "You did a great job with the ornaments!"

"Yes, it's gorgeous!" Windsong reached for a poinsettia from the table centerpiece and handed it to Sailor. "You're a diva, my darling."

Sailor lowered her head and blushed.

Forest and I looked at each other. "Um, we had an incident or two."

"Yeah," Forest added. "First, Ranger Rick chewed us out for putting lights on the tree out front and then that old Hank guy yelled at us just for being outside."

GB took a drink of milk. "Hmm, well it sounds like we could certainly use a more cheerful holiday spirit around here. Unfortunately, this might make it worse—we decided to decline Audrey's offer and will place a bid on that old fixer-upper in Brussels, instead."

"Why don't we get a say in it?" Sailor protested.

Windsong patted GB's hand. "Bobby, I think you should tell everyone what happened at the cabin."

"I hate to sound like I'm off my rocker, but for the sake of safety, you should know." GB's voice shook as he continued. "This afternoon I drank Audrey's tea. It was right after that when I was examining the living room walls for signs of compromise in the plaster, that I glanced up at the portrait of Audrey's deceased Uncle Vincent. I was positive the eyes moved in my direction."

"Grandpa, what are you saying? Do you think the tea is poisoned?" I pushed my plate away, suddenly feeling sick to my stomach.

"I don't know for sure, but don't drink that woman's tea under any circumstances." GB shook his finger at us.

"Please, I don't want you to worry," Windsong said. "It's probably not the tea. I drank two cups of it and didn't hallucinate."

Just then the lights went out. An eerie moaning sound arose from the basement.

"Did you hear that?" GB stood to his feet.

Windsong grabbed his hand. "I heard it, hon."

"We heard it!" Sadie glanced at Bert. "We probably should've told you … we heard strange noises before you even got here. Bert said we shouldn't tell you, because it was probably just dementia on our part."

Bert took a long drink from his glass of water. "Okay, okay. We heard music and laughter, but after Windsong read the lightkeeper's account, we figured it was the ghosts of John Craig and Carrie Spencer." He looked down in shame. "We figured these were happy hauntings, like Casper the Friendly Ghost. It didn't seem like cause for alarm."

"Grandpa, we heard a ghost, too!" Sailor's hands flung across the table, which toppled her glass of apple cider over the burgundy tablecloth.

"It's true," Forest chimed in. "I heard the floorboards creaking in the night."

GB stroked his goatee. "I have to say, I don't know what to make of all this. If it wasn't the tea, then what in tarnation is going on here?"

"Grandpa, I know you don't believe in ghosts, but is it possible you could be wrong?" I asked. "Maybe we should try to get in touch with Quinn so he can help figure things out?"

"Well, if it will make you feel better," GB said. "Right now, I think I'm going to turn in for the night."

"Goodnight, Grandpa. Hopefully your head clears by morning." I got up to leave the table and motioned for Forest and Sailor to follow me.

"Let's head to the sitting room."

"Great idea," Forest said. "I like sitting."

The three of us regrouped on the couch to go over the latest findings.

"What we have here is a case of stolen paintings, mysterious tracks that lead to the lighthouse, and a few ghosts on the loose."

"What's this all about?" Sailor pulled her ponytail out of the green scrunchie and neatly redid her hair into a bun.

"You're out of the loop, Sailor," Forest said. "All this time you spent making cookies with Sadie, Dominic and I have been working on a case." He leaned back, a smile of satisfaction on his face.

"Being that as it may," I shot a warning look at Forest, "we are going to need all hands-on deck for this whopper of a mystery."

Forest sneered in Sailor's direction. "Exactly. We need help, as in … brain power. Sorry sis, but when God was handing out brains, you thought He said 'trains,' and asked for a slow one."

I cleared my throat. "Need I remind you, if it weren't for Sailor's input in the circus show mystery last summer, we wouldn't have solved that case?"

Forest held up his palms. "Okay, okay. I guess you were somewhat helpful."

"Come on, clue me in!" Sailor begged.

"Fine, but first, I need something." I started rummaging through my backpack.

"What do you need?" Forest leaned forward. "A compass? A calculator?"

"Aha! Here it is." I pulled the bag of Cheetos out and ripped it open.

We all grabbed a handful before continuing.

"Let's start with the fact that before we even got here, Bert and Sadie were hearing noises. Then we heard a few ourselves."

"Definitely," Forest added. "Floorboards creaking, laughing, and music."

"And another thing. There were footprints that led to this building and Forest saw a man out there in the middle of the night. Ghosts don't leave footprints."

"Well, what about the cabin lady who sees dead people?" Forest kicked off his shoes. "And the freaky eyes that were moving in that painting?"

"Gross! Put your shoes back on." Sailor wrinkled her nose.

"Pay attention, Sailor, so we can bring you up to speed." I wiped off my mouth with the back of my hand. "When we went to Audrey's cabin, she told Windsong a book flew off the shelf, and she thought she saw her dead uncle."

"Whoa!" Sailor pressed her hands to her cheeks.

"It seems that Schroeder's, the cabin, and this lighthouse are all connected somehow … wait a minute." I reached into my backpack again.

"What are you looking for now? Doritos?" Forest teased.

"Very funny. No, I forgot to tell you guys, but I found this note stuck in a chair cushion at Schroeder's." I licked the Cheeto dust off my fingers and pulled out the paper from the inside pocket of my backpack.

"Look at this list: Schroeder's, Library, Hemlock Lane, and Rawley Point. Audrey's cabin is on Hemlock Lane, and Rawley Point is the location of this lighthouse. Some of these locations seem to be haunted."

"Let me see." Forest grabbed the piece of paper. "Okay, but what about the library?"

Before I could ponder his question, my phone began to vibrate on the end table. The notification bar read: CAPTAIN QUINN.

"Hold that thought," I said to Forest while I scrambled to answer the call.

"Hello, this is Dominic …"

CHAPTER 7

"Dominic, I have news for you," Quinn announced. "I was just called out to an emergency at the Lester Public Library. They thought they had a ghost knocking books off of shelves and displacing things."

"Are you serious!" I turned on the speaker so Forest and Sailor could hear.

"Affirmative—and a few of their wall hangings are missing, too—some valuable portraits by some local dude. Anyway, I can't make heads or tails out of it, and thought you might have a clue."

"We're working on it," I replied.

"Excellent." Quinn's voice started to cut out. "I'm picking up interference from my radar, but before I go there's one more thing …"

"What's that, Captain?"

The phone started to crackle.

"I reviewed the video footage from the Schroeder's building and discovered the apparition you captured wasn't a ghost—it was a drone," Quinn responded just as his phone cut out, ending the call.

"I think we have the answers we need." I put down the phone and went back to the piece of notepaper. "Now we know how the library is connected. Someone is stealing artwork and Rawley point is next."

Sailor leaned in for a closer look. "We need to find out who made the list."

"This is written on stationery. See the green and black text in the upper left corner?" I pointed. "It's ripped, but you can still make out the words 'Co. Inc.' It looks like a business name."

"Maybe it's Schroeder's!" Sailor shouted.

"Yeah, right, Sailor," Forest scowled.

"She's on to something." I reached for my cell phone again and typed "Schroeder's" into the Google search bar. "There it is, 'SCHROEDER BROS. CO. INC' with the exact same lettering." I held the paper out to them. "What does that tell you?"

"The Schroeder brothers are crooks?" Sailor said.

"Close, but no cigar." I folded the paper and tossed it into my backpack. "This could've been written by a Schroeder's employee."

"I put all my money on Glen," Sailor interrupted. "Never trust a guy wearing a vest."

"About the only thing that vest will do is protect him from women," Forest joked. "But if you ask me, Hank is number one on the list. He's been hanging around the cabin, he refused to drink Audrey's tea, and he got awfully grumpy when he saw us by the tower. And Ranger Rick is on the list, too."

"Come on, Forest. I know in the past we suspected him, but in the end his name was always cleared."

"Maybe this time we'll get lucky." Forest had a wild look in his eyes.

"So, what's the game plan?" Sailor got up from the couch and looked out the frosted window.

I crumpled the empty Cheetos bag and launched it into the garbage can. "We need to head to Schroeder's to find out whose stationery the note was written on. It's our best lead to finding the stolen art."

The next morning, I awoke to a foreboding dark sky. I reached for my phone. 8:30 am. Forest was still sleeping, so I quickly threw on my flannel shirt and jeans and headed downstairs where I found GB fumbling with the Keurig machine. I knew better than to start any important conversation before he had his coffee, but I had a pressing question.

"Good morning, Dominic!"

I rubbed the sleep from my eyes. "Hey, Grandpa. Did you change your mind about the cabin?"

"Nope." The coffee gadget finally spit out a cup of coffee, which he grabbed and took to the table. "What are you kids planning for today? It's Christmas Eve, you know."

"Well, actually that's what I wanted to ask you about." I grabbed the carton of chocolate milk from the fridge. "We want to go into town for some last-minute Christmas shopping," I lied.

"I'd love to take you, but Audrey is coming for lunch. Windsong and I need to break the news that the sale is off. We're feeling a little spooked about all this."

"In that case, could we take your truck? Forest has his license now, and he'd be careful with it."

GB glanced out the window. "Sorry, Dominic, but it snowed last night. I just can't take a chance with you kids navigating Fireball on these slippery roads."

Windsong sauntered into the kitchen in her nightgown and slippers just in time to hear the last bit of conversation. "What's this? You need a ride into town?" She yawned as she opened the kitchen cabinet for a clean coffee mug. "Ranger Sally is meeting up with a few locals to do some Christmas caroling in Two Rivers. Would you want to catch a ride with her?"

Ughhh. Not really.

"Sure."

And that's how Forest, Sailor and I found ourselves crammed into Ranger Sally's truck, along with her friends that she picked up along the way.

The gray-haired lady in a purple knit cap who

sat next to me was overly plump. I tried to move away, but there wasn't an inch to spare. Her lilac air freshener perfume was giving me a headache.

"Say, did you kids ever see the movie, *It's a Wonderful Life?*" Sally glanced back in our direction.

"Of course," Forest shot back. "It's a classic. Everybody's seen it."

Sally stopped at the red light on Main Street. "Yes, of course. But you can't miss the impact of that story. You know, the difference one person's life can have in this world."

"Well, yeah. Without George Bailey, there's nightclubs and casinos … it's awesome! Makes me wish he never *had* been born."

Sally frowned. It looked like she was going to say something, but instead she began to belt out a Christmas tune. Some of the other ladies joined in.

That's Forest. He makes friends wherever he goes.

After a few out-of-tune rounds of "Deck the Halls," we were finally dropped off at Schroeder's.

"I'll text you when we're heading back," Sally

shouted from the driver side window before barreling down Main Street with the Christmas carolers.

The three of us hurried into Schroeder's.

"There he is." Forest pointed out Glen, who was taking care of a customer by the winter boot display. He sported a red and green vest with a Santa Claus tie. *Nice.*

While Glen's back was turned, I rifled through a pile of papers on his desk. Nothing abnormal there, except a creepy picture of Glen in an apron, holding a platter of tacos.

I opened the desk drawer. A full pad of SCHROEDER BROS. stationery. *How do you like me now?*

"Hurry up, Dominic!" Forest hissed.

"Hold on, almost done." I glanced down at the trash can next to his desk and found a pile of "Open House" flyers. I looked closely at the address. 127 Hemlock Lane. And the invitation date was December 28th. Four days away. That was Audrey's cabin. Why were these in the garbage?

After Glen finished helping his customers, he headed our way. "You again."

"I really like your Christmas outfit," Sailor said.

"Thanks, kid, but I'm busy. What do you need?" He motioned us over to his desk.

I stepped up and placed the stationary page flat on top. "Sorry to bother you, but can you tell me if this list looks familiar, by chance?" I asked.

He took a quick glance. "Nope. Never saw it before," he responded before returning to a stack of shoe boxes gathered for inventory.

"Are you sure, because I noticed the paper matches your note pad, here?" I pointed to the paper.

"We all use the same stationery. It's part of our office supplies."

"Uh, okay. What about these flyers?" I fanned them out in front of him. "Did you throw them in the trash?" I asked.

"Never saw those before, either."

Well, that went nowhere.

"Okay. Do you know where Julia is?" I asked.

Glen shrugged his shoulders. "She's on her break. Probably in the coffee shop with her boyfriend." And with that he straightened his tie and walked away.

We headed back to the front of the store where I saw Julia at a corner table, huddled close to an older man with a black mustache and goatee wearing a grey wool cap. As we approached, he gave us a withering stare.

Julia placed her hand on the man's shoulder. "Max, I'd like you to meet our famous ghostbuster detectives … She looked at us with a blank stare. "I'm sorry, I forgot your names."

"Uh, I'm Dominic and this is Forest and Sailor."

"Well, those are names you don't hear every day. Detectives, eh?" He smiled blandly at us. I couldn't help but notice his large, curved nose. It looked like a hawk's beak.

"Well, we're not famous or anything," Forest added. "It's more like something we do for fun." He shoved his hands in his pockets.

"We were hoping to get some information here, but Glen was too busy to talk to us," Sailor complained.

Julia sipped her coffee. "Sorry about that. It's our busy time of the year, you know."

"We were just wondering if you lost this note?" I pulled the list from my pocket and laid it on the table.

They leaned in to scan the piece of paper and gave each other a blank stare. Julia picked up her coffee cup, spilling some onto the note.

Did she do that on purpose?

"Just what are you getting at, kid?" Max snarled.

Julia put her cup back down. "I'm sorry, but it looks like we've had a little … *accident*." She cleaned everything up with a napkin, including the evidence.

Max gave us the evil eye. That was our cue to leave.

We hurried to the door and headed outside, where Sally and her choir group were approaching around the corner, singing a hearty chorus of "Rocking Around the Christmas Tree." The wind picked up; a string of lights hanging across the street began clanging together.

I zipped up my hood. "Do you think Julia's boyfriend looks familiar?" I asked Forest.

"No. Why do you ask?"

"I don't know. He reminds me of those thugs from New York we ran into on our first case at the campground. He just looks very familiar." I pulled out my cellphone. "Do you remember that Audrey said her dead uncle was buried in a cemetery nearby?"

"Yeah," Forest said. "And?"

"I think we should look for his gravestone."

I googled nearby cemeteries on my cell phone.

"Looks like Lakeview Cemetery is the only one near Point Beach." I held out my phone to show him the map.

"I'm still not sure what it is you're hoping to find in a cemetery," Forest said.

"I'm hoping to find a ghost for real this time."

CHAPTER 8

A rusty, iron gate stood guard to a small cemetery ensconced deep in the woods. The tall pine trees drooped with frosted ice and the gravestones were covered in snow. The prospect of finding Vincent's grave seemed daunting.

"Brrr … how long will this take?" Sailor's steamy breath circled the air as she huddled close to us, trying to keep warm.

A north wind suddenly picked up, blowing the mounds of snow off a few tree branches. That gave me an idea.

"We need to clear the gravestones so we can read the names. Forest, you take the left row of stones. Sailor, you take the middle and I'll take the right."

I had just begun wiping the snow off the headstones in my section, when I came across something sticking out of the ground—a bright red color on one of the burial plots. I reached down and pulled it up. A single red rose.

Someone was recently here. I brushed off the dusting of snow over the gravestone.

In loving memory
Vincent Anthony Hart
1967 –
So valiant in your voyage
The angst of death unknown
The angels carry onward
Where scattered seeds have sown.

"Guys—I think I found our ghost!"

Sailor and Forest trudged their way through the knee-deep snow in my direction.

"I'm confused. How is this dead guy a ghost?" Forest asked.

"Because he's not dead." I cleared away the rest of the snow on the gravestone. "What year did he die?"

"Ooh, now I see," Sailor gasped, "… he didn't!"

She pulled her pink stocking cap down tightly over her ears.

I stood back. "Not only that, I think I know who he is."

"Geez, Dominic. Did you have Wheaties for breakfast? What's the deal?"

"Okay, okay. That Max guy looked familiar. I recognized his hooked nose. Don't you see? He's Vincent! He's older and his hair is dyed black, but it's definitely him."

"Huh." Forest pushed his bangs out of his eyes. "Let me guess … he's the art thief."

"Game, set, match." I set the rose down where I found it. "Something else has been bothering me, and this sort of ties it all together. Remember Audrey said Julia was a good friend of hers? But according to Julia, Audrey is cuckoo for Cocoa Puffs."

"So?" Forest was getting impatient.

I couldn't blame him. We were colder than penguins at the North Pole.

"So, Julia is throwing Audrey under the bus.

She's conspiring with Vincent to steal her artwork. Does that sound like something a friend would do?"

"Dude." Forest got quiet.

"Strap on your skis. If Audrey is still at the lighthouse, this would be a good time to check out the situation at her cabin."

"So … we're snooping?" Sailor gave a lopsided grin.

"Uh, yep."

When we reached the cabin, I breathed a sigh of relief to see Audrey's car wasn't there.

I found the key under the fake rock where Audrey left it, and we went inside where we were greeted by the smoky aroma from the embers of the wood-burning fireplace.

"That feels nice and warm." Sailor rubbed her hands over her arms. "Where to?"

"The basement." I led the way.

"The cold, scary basement …?" Forest joked.

At the bottom of the stairs, we passed a few wooden easels with partially finished canvases along with pastels and oil paints arranged in trays on drop cloths.

I headed right to the south wall with the covered window and started pushing the space in front of it. Nothing gave way, but as I continued to walk along the wall, a panel shifted, revealing a hidden staircase behind it.

"Well, how do you do?" Forest leaned into the walkway.

We gingerly climbed the creaky steps, pushing aside cobwebs along the stairwell. When we reached the top, a small crawl space to the left led to a wall that I assumed was behind the fireplace, given that the wall was warm to the touch.

"What's this?" Forest pushed on two circled indentations. The holes opened, and he peeked through.

"I do believe we're standing behind Vincent's

portrait," Forest said as he pulled himself back. "This is how he spies on Audrey."

"I wanna see!" Sailor whined.

"Go on, but hurry!" I pushed open the holes and held them down so she could get a good look.

To the right, another tight wall space led to a dead end. I pushed on that wall and was able to reach my hand through to what felt like a row of books.

"So, this is how he pushed a book off the shelf to scare Audrey!"

I inched back to the eyeholes for another look. Suddenly the front door opened. Audrey was back. I motioned for the others to keep quiet.

Audrey headed to the kitchen. "Oh, there you are my little snowball!" She must've been referring to Socrates. Then I heard water running from the faucet. When she turned off the water, there was a clanking sound, probably from setting teacups on the table.

A knocking came at the front door.

Not good. She had company.

Audrey scurried to open it.

"Well, Julia, what a pleasant surprise!" She offered her a seat on the couch. "I was just putting on some tea. Would you care for a cup?"

Julia pulled off her knitted hat and shook her dark curls loose. "Uh, no thanks. I heard you had a bad experience with your homemade tea."

"Where did you hear that?" Audrey seemed to take offense. "For your information, someone planted hemlock in my greenhouse. I did not plant that!"

"Relax, my dear friend. I completely believe you. Someone is out to get you." Julia patted Audrey's hand.

"Out to get me?" Audrey stood to her feet. "Well why on earth would anyone have a problem with *me*?"

"Sshh, calm down, Audrey." Julia placed a finger on her lips. "You're overreacting. Maybe you should switch to decaffeinated tea."

"Who's that???" Audrey ran to the window, her expression darkening. "It's … it's … Vincent!"

Julia looked out the window. "I don't see him, honey. You must be imagining things."

"Right there—can't you see him! He's right in front of the pine tree." Audrey grabbed Julia's hand and pulled her closer to the window.

"No, I'm sorry. No one is there. I really think you should go to the hospital. You're presenting signs of a breakdown. I'm worried about you, Audrey."

From my eyehole view, I could clearly see Vince standing outside the window. What was she trying to pull?

RRrr--AAeee--ERrr!

Socrates jumped up on the mantle and swiped at the eyeholes, sending the urn of ashes clattering to the floor.

I jumped back and motioned for Forest and Sailor to follow me back down the steps.

"What now?" Sailor whispered.

I looked upward. "We need to get out of here."

CHAPTER 9

We waited in the dark basement for what seemed like an eternity. When Audrey finally escorted Julia to her car, we made a mad dash up the stairs and out the back door.

After quickly strapping on our skis, we pushed ourselves down the trail at breakneck speed—well, as fast as we could go with Sailor tripping at every turn. By the time we reached the lighthouse, I barely noticed the wind chill. I was sweating profusely under my fleece jacket.

As we neared the house, we could hear loud music, and Sprinkles was barking his head off.

Since it was already Christmas Eve, we needed to wrap up this mystery, and soon. We would need some peace and quiet for that.

"I know you won't be thrilled to see another basement, but right now that's the only place where we can get some privacy."

The three of us went in the back door and descended the basement steps. I tugged on a string that hung from a lightbulb on the ceiling. The dark room lit up, revealing white plastered walls lined with rows of conduit and exposed pipes fastened to the length of the unfinished ceiling.

There was a small table and chairs in the corner. We sat down and took the opportunity to regroup.

Sailor tore off her stocking cap and put her hands over her face. "I have never been so scared in my life!"

"What about the time when that lumberjack locked us in the bunker?" Forest said.

"Not helping, Forest." I shot him the stink eye. "Okay, so a lot has happened today." I grabbed a Baja Blast from my backpack and took a big drink. "Who do you think is behind this?"

"I think it's Vincent, or Max, or whatever he calls himself, and Hank and Julia," Forest said.

"I wouldn't rule out Glen." I pulled out the "Open House" flyer from my pocket. "He claims he never saw these, but I'm not sure I believe him."

"So what?" Sailor raised an eyebrow.

"Well, obviously Audrey asked him to put up the flyers. Instead, he threw them in the garbage."

My theory was greeted with silence.

"Guys, come on! Don't you see what's going on?" I raised my hands in the air. "There's a conspiracy against Audrey. Someone is stealing her paintings, trying to make her look insane, and apparently putting the kibosh on her cabin sale."

"Okay, that does sound suspicious," Sailor admitted. "But who would do that. And why?"

"I don't know just yet."

On a hunch, I flipped over my phone and typed "Vincent Hart, Two Rivers, WI" into my search bar.

"Hey, listen to this! It's a Herald Times newspaper article from 2017." I scrolled down as I read the headline story:

Vincent A. Hart, a local Two Rivers man has been charged with suspicion of grand theft and embezzlement for allegedly absconding with $210,000 from Maritime Finan-

I was getting excited. "Don't you see? He was on
his way to prison. In order to get out of it, he faked his
own death."

"Booya! Emphasis on the 'boo.'" Forest slapped
me on the back.

"I don't know about you guys, but I really
worked up an appetite. Let's grab a snack and then we
can decide what our next move is."

Just then, a text message came in on my phone.

*Hey kids. Where are you? We need to do some last-
minute Christmas shopping. Heading out with the Buckleys.
Won't be home until late. Windsong.*

"Perfect! Let's head upstairs. I'm starving." As I
reached for my backpack to put my phone away, I
knocked something off a shelf by the wall.

"Well, what do we have here?" As I bent down
to pick up what looked like a tape recorder, I realized it
was actually a sound effects machine. I grabbed my

phone and held the light over the labels on the keys.

"Moaning, laughing, screaming, music, stairs creaking …" I pressed the "laughing" button. An eerie, high-pitched laughing sound rose from the recorder.

"Hey," Sailor shouted, "that's the same laugh I heard the other night!"

Forest reached past me and pressed the "stairs creaking" button. An eerie creaking noise sounded from the recorder. "I heard that before," he confirmed.

"So, whoever it is comes down here, selects a tune, and it's piped upstairs."

Sailor tried to force open a stubborn cock-eyed desk drawer, causing it to slip off the track. As she jostled it back into place, the bottom separated, revealing a secret compartment underneath.

"What do you think this is?" A small stainless-steel canister slid toward the front.

"I'm pretty sure it's a time capsule," Forest said. "Open it up and see if anything's inside."

She swiveled the lid, reached in, and pulled out a sketch of a brick lighthouse and keeper's building.

"Cool. I bet it's another one of those treasure maps like the one Roaring Dan the pirate had."

"I don't think so. This looks like a blueprint." I took a closer look. "The inscription at the top reads: 'Twin River Point, 1874.' This must be what the original building and lighthouse looked like before the fire."

"Maybe it will help explain how our 'ghost' gets in here undetected—unless it really can walk through walls," Forest said.

"You're a genius!" I studied the print. "It's a long shot, but if my suspicions are correct, this is the spot." I pointed to a structure that led out of the building from underground, but when I walked over to the actual wall in the basement, there was nothing there but cheap paneling.

"That's funny. According to the design, there should be a doorway here," I said to the others. On a hunch, I ran my hands along the paneling. "Wait a minute … this one's loose."

Forest helped me slide it back a step, revealing

an old wooden door. I tried the handle. It wouldn't budge. "That stinks—the door's locked." I ran my hands through my hair. "But maybe we can get in from the outside?"

"No way, uh-uh." Sailor crossed her arms. "You two are on your own. I'll wait here in case you run into trouble."

"Then stand guard with this." I handed her a can of Deep Woods Off bug repellant from the shelf.

After Forest and I threw on our coats and boots, I opened the door, letting in a blast of cold air. By this time, it was pitch black outside, and the house was dark. The others must still be gone shopping.

The moon illuminated the way, and it was a good thing, because the flashlights that GB gets from the Dollar Tree really don't work very well. We headed over to the exact location on the outside of the rental building, and sure enough—there was a cellar door.

"Why didn't we see this before?" I bent down and brushed off the snow around the padlock. "Hey— it's open! It looks like someone used a bolt cutter."

Forest and I pulled back the trap door a crack and shined our lights through the opening onto stone walls covered with moss and webs. A wooden shipping container sat on the floor.

"We're not going in there, are we?" Forest rubbed the back of his neck. "I mean, what if it's booby-trapped?"

"Come on, scaredy-cat. Don't you want to see what's inside?" I dangled my legs over the ledge, leaped down into the opening, and landed with a thud in front of the large crate. Without wasting any time, I pulled open the cover.

"You've gotta be kidding." Forest peered over my shoulder at the stacks of paintings and rolled up prints.

"This is what the crooks must be smuggling." I lifted up a painting of a beach scene. "Some of these are Audrey's." I shined my light on the signature at the bottom of each one. "And Lester Bentley's!"

Not too far off, the sound of an engine roared across the snow. I quickly put the lid back on and peered over the ledge to see what all the commotion was. A beam of light from a snowmobile streamed in our direction. It was getting closer.

"Someone's coming our way!" I warned Forest. We closed the trap door overhead, holding it shut from the inside. The engine grew louder and louder, stopping right outside the cellar. Someone scuffled over and tried to pull on the door while Forest and I held it down with all our strength.

"It must be frozen shut," I heard a man say after giving up. *It was Vincent.*

"Now what?" A woman muttered. "We don't have much time. The renters could return any minute, and I think those kids are onto us."

That had to be Julia.

"First, I need to get a pry bar," Vince said. "In the meantime, you can head up to the tower and signal the boat. Then we stick to the plan. I get the paintings loaded onto the sled. You take care of intruders."

"Aye-aye, Captain."

Their voices dissipated.

"Phew, that was close!" I said to Forest.

"Yeah — I thought we were gonners, for sure."

We released our grip on the door when a blood-curdling shriek came from inside the basement. I recognized that scream … it was from the sound effects machine. *Or was it?*

CHAPTER 10

"Dominic, Forest, help!" Sailor's voice sounded muffled coming from the other side of the cellar door that led to the basement. I burst through the door.

"Sailor!" I yelled. "We're coming!"

There she was, cornered by Hank, fending him off with the can of bug spray.

He raised his long, burly arms and tried to hold her down and block the spray.

"What are you doing?" Forest lurched toward Hank. "Leave her alone!"

Hank stepped back in retreat. I noticed he was holding a key. "I knew you kids were in trouble, so I came to get you out."

"How did you know we were down here?" I narrowed my eyes at him. "And why would we trust you?"

"Because I've been keeping track of what's going

on around here and it's my conclusion that this light house is being used for some kind of illegal activity." He closed the cellar door on the inside and locked it before replacing the paneling.

"You're right," Forest said. "They're hiding paintings in there and Vince is coming back for them at any minute—something about a boat they're signaling from the tower."

"In that case," Hank said, "I need to stop them. You kids stay here."

The three of us looked at each other and followed him outside. We had come this far in the mystery; we had to see it through.

Torrents of snow and sleet pelted my skin as I watched the lighthouse signal lamp pierce through the darkened sky. It flashed across the lake where I caught a glimpse of a hovercraft waiting offshore.

A shadowy figure looked out from the tower, directing the beam of light onto the open water. It had to be Julia. On the horizon, I heard the low rumble of a snowmobile. It was heading toward the craft.

"We're too late. Vince must've already loaded the paintings onto that sled," I told the others. To our surprise, the snowmobile hit an ice shove with a jolt, causing the driver to launch head over heels and get knocked unconscious.

"Now's our chance!" I led them toward the sled to retrieve the paintings.

Out of nowhere, the ghoulish image of a luminescent creature circled above us.

"There it is again!" Sailor pointed before the ghostly menace made a swooping pass, catching us off guard as we ducked to the ground just in time.

"Run for cover!" I shouted. Bounding through the deep snow, the three of us separated during the pursuit. Forest and Sailor reached the woods and hid from sight, but I found myself all alone—right on the edge of Lake Michigan.

Beneath the snow, I heard it—*Crack!*

My heart beat out of my chest as I tried to remember what to do in a situation like this. Instinct told me to lay down flat to distribute my weight over the thin ice. But every time I tried to drag myself toward shore, the wind kept pushing me further backward. Soon, I'd be close to open water.

"Hang on kid, I'm coming for you!" Hank yelled. He had a long rope in his hand which he tossed in my direction. I had to use my last bit of strength to reach out for it and hold on.

With the snowmobile shifted in reverse, Hank was able to pull me to safety while the waves crashed against the ice with a vengeance.

When we got back to shore, Ranger Rick stood waiting on the bank, his hands on his hips. "Just what are you trying to pull, Nimrod?"

Hank turned toward the ranger and scowled. "These kids caught the art thieves red-handed. Where were you while this was going on right under your nose?"

Steam blew out of the ranger's ears. "Now, listen here, you glorified janitor. I was just in the process of wrapping things up. Nothing gets past me."

"Fine," Hank shot back. "Well, grab your handcuffs, my know-it-all friend. Bonnie and Clyde are ready to check in to the Crowbar Hotel."

"Thanks, Hank. I owe you one." I collapsed just as Forest and Sailor ran to my side.

"I'm so glad you're alright!" Sailor kissed me on the cheek. "And look, we solved the mystery and caught the ghosts."

I turned my head to see that Hank had Vincent tied up with the rope. "What about Julia?"

"She was up in the lighthouse controlling the ghostly drone that was after us until Hank locked the door, trapping her inside the tower," Forest said. "She's not going anywhere unless her name's Rapunzel."

In the distance, I could make out the outline of GB's red truck coming up the drive. The three of us stood, waving our arms to flag him down. He stopped short to let Bert out.

"The ship! It's here … it's here!" Bert held his binoculars in hand. "Captain Santa's here!"

Ranger Rick ran alongside Bert to the shoreline

and grabbed his binoculars. He peered over the dark, murky waters. "I see it! I see the ghost ship!"

I caught up to them and looked in the same direction, but what I saw was no phantom ship … it was real. The hovercraft lifted, pausing a few seconds before taking off into the night.

"That was a hovercraft," I explained.

"No, no. Look further out. It's the ghost ship!" Bert took the binoculars from the ranger and handed them to me. "See it? It's loaded with evergreen trees." He pointed toward the east.

I looked again but all I saw was a patch of fog.

Bert slapped the ranger on the back. "Well, that certainly was a Christmas miracle, I tell you what."

Ranger Rick stood speechless.

If the ranger ended up believing in Santa now, that really would be a miracle.

After breakfast we said goodbye to the Buckleys, who left to spend the rest of the holiday with their family. Once we finished packing and were ready to go, the five of us gathered around the Christmas tree.

Suddenly, there was a knock at the door. Sailor ran to answer it and came back with Audrey.

"Merry Christmas!" Audrey slipped off her scarf and shook the snow off it. "I was hoping to catch you before you left. Ranger Rick called and said Vince and Julia were escorted to the Manitowoc County jail. They won't see the light of day anytime soon."

"What about the hovercraft driver that Dominic saw?" Forest leaned forward in his seat.

"Oh, well they haven't found him yet. But thank God he didn't get away with any of the paintings." Julia frowned as she took a seat on the couch.

"Anyway, I wanted to thank you kids for everything you did. If it weren't for you, Vince would've taken over my cabin, and I'd be in a mental ward somewhere, or dead, due to hemlock poisoning."

"You're shivering, dear. Let me grab you a warm

drink." Windsong went to the kitchen and came back with a steaming cup of chai tea.

"So, why did Vince want your cabin?" GB asked.

Audrey pulled off her mittens and took the cup from Windsong. "Is there anything in here I should worry about?" She looked up and smiled.

We all laughed at that comment.

"Vincent's father built that cabin, and Vince grew up there. That's how he knew about the secret wall in the living room. Apparently, his dad added the hiding place in case they were invaded. He was a PTSD survivor of WWII." She took a sip of tea. "Anyway, Vince was furious that Granddad gave the cabin to me. But Vince had faked his death, so what did he expect?"

"And how exactly did he do that?" I asked.

"Have you ever heard of the Great Lakes Triangle?" she asked. "They claim there were more planes gone missing over Lake Michigan than there was in the Bermuda Triangle."

I nodded. "We heard. Bert told us about that."

"Vince had his pilot's license. His flight from

Michigan was scheduled to arrive at the Manitowoc County airport five years ago. It never came."

"Well, what about the urn on your mantle?" Forest leaned forward in his seat.

"Oh, that. Just burnt ashes from the fireplace. I know that sounds silly, but that and the gravestone at the cemetery helped bring closure. I mean, we had to assume he was dead." Her eyes misted.

Sailor took a seat next to Audrey and reached for her hand. "Do you know why he and Julia were stealing all those paintings that we found in the cellar?"

Audrey leaned forward. "Vincent was so angry after he found out I owned the cabin. He became determined to even the score by stealing all of my paintings, and Lester Bentley's too, since Bentley was my mentor, and then poisoning me to prove I was unstable so he could get the cabin back. It was a case of the 'green-eyed monster' at work."

Windsong grew quiet for a minute. "You might find this interesting," she said. "Hank stopped in yesterday, and we had a long talk. Turns out he started the fire here back in 1962, and then got scared and ran off, not to return until two years ago when he took the groundskeeper job at the light house."

Audrey's jaw dropped. "I didn't know that!"

"It's true. Do you see the irony? There were two men who faked their deaths because they committed a crime. One man came back to continue his shady activity, and the other came back and redeemed himself."

"Well, my goodness!" Audrey looked down into her cup. "It seems almost … biblical, when you think about it." She looked up and smiled. "But enough about that. I brought you kids a present." She reached into her purse and handed me a small box wrapped in red paper with a green bow, winking at GB and Windsong.

Sailor grabbed it from me and tore off the paper. Inside the box was a key.

"We bought Audrey's cabin!" Windsong squeezed GB's hand. Their smiles said it all.

"Really?" Sailor said. "I'm so happy we won't have to vacation in Algoma. Now that we scared off the ghosts, it's going to be great around here."

"And the first thing I'm going to do after we move is to fix that crack in the foundation," GB added.

The three of us had to laugh. *If only he knew.* But we all were thrilled at the news.

"Wait, there's one more gift under the tree and the tag says it's from Hank." Forest reached for a present wrapped in sparkling blue paper and opened it. "It's the time capsule!"

"We should start collecting things to put in it. That way we can bury it when we come back to Point Beach in the summer," Sailor suggested.

"You might want to throw in a pair of underwear for Dominic while you're at it." Forest tossed the stainless-steel container to me. There was a note inside. I pulled it out:

I couldn't forgive myself back in 1962. I thought the easiest way was to disappear rather than face what I had done when I set that fire. Thank you for giving me a chance to redeem myself. I trust you with my secret.

Sincerely, Hank.

I looked up. "He really was a good guy after all."

After Audrey left, we grabbed our bags and headed to the truck. Once everyone was settled inside, GB turned on the radio and tuned in to WOMT.

"I'd like to welcome back to 'Be Our Guest' this morning, Quinn from SCI-FI-WI, here with us to report on his recent ghost hunt in Two Rivers."

"Thank you," Quinn said. *"Unfortunately, I couldn't find any ghosts, but I can honestly say that this town definitely has some strange phenomena going around. I left that for three of the best detectives to deal with. I'd say that with all the stunts these local yokels try to pull around here, they'll have a busy future ahead of them."*

"And what does the future hold for you?" the radio host asked Quinn.

"I'm thinking about switching gears and becoming a storm chaser. Being in the eye of the storm is where the action is!"

"Indeed — and we certainly had a doozy recently! Best of luck to you." The announcer signed off.

"Don't go getting any crazy ideas." Grandpa Bob

eyed me from the rear-view mirror.

"Nothing to worry about, Grandpa. I think I'll stick to being a detective."

As we drove down the road, I stared out the window, reflecting on our many adventures at Point Beach.

The storm had lifted, leaving behind early rays of sunlight shimmering off the water of Lake Michigan. All was still and peaceful until a wave rushed up to shore, carrying with it—an ice-covered hemlock tree.

Maybe Captain Santa came after all …

Debby lives in Maribel, Wisconsin. She's a member of Pens of Praise Christian writers' group and enjoys family gatherings, country life and the four seasons.

Kate lives in Branch, Wisconsin. She's a member of Pens of Praise Christian writers' group and a church accompanist. She enjoys spending time with her family.

Connect with us online at:

Facebook.com/MysteryatPointBeach

Facebook.com/TheTinCanSeries

Our thanks to the Lord, who makes all things possible, and to Sarah Grosskopf and Anne Bender our beta readers and biggest fans.

Books in the Mystery at Point Beach Series:

Book 1: Sundae Wars

Book 2: Pirate's Booty

Book 3: Alien Invasion

Book 4: Bushwhacked

Book 5: The Ringmaster

Book 6: Haunted Hemlock

Books in The Tin Can Series:

Book 1: Mystery at Flamingo Bay